The Rock Maiden

A Chinese Tale of Love and Loyalty

Written by Natasha Yim

Illustrated by Pirkko Vainio

Wisdom Tales

The Rock Maiden: A Chinese Tale of Love and Loyalty
Text © 2017 Natasha Yim
Illustrations © 2017 Pirkko Vainio

Wisdom Tales is an imprint of World Wisdom, Inc.

Library of Congress Cataloging-in-Publication Data

Names: Yim, Natasha. | Vainio, Pirkko, illustrator.
Title: The rock maiden : a Chinese tale of love and loyalty / by Natasha Yim
; illustrated by Pirkko Vainio.
Description: Bloomington, Indiana : Wisdom Tales, [2017] | Based on the
Chinese legend of Amah Rock. | Summary: When her husband goes missing, a
new mother pleads with Tin Hau, the patron goddess of fisherman, for help.
Identifiers: LCCN 2016038502 (print) | LCCN 2016046491 (ebook) | ISBN
9781937786656 (casebound : alk. paper) | ISBN 9781937786663 (epub)
Subjects: | CYAC: Folklore--China--Hong Kong
Classification: LCC PZ8.1.Y55 Ro 2017 (print) | LCC PZ8.1.Y55 (ebook) | DDC
398.2 [E] --dc23
LC record available at https://lccn.loc.gov/2016038502

Printed in China on acid-free paper.

Production Date: October 2016
Plant & Location: Printed by 1010 Printing International Ltd.,
Job/Batch#: TT16100042

For information address Wisdom Tales,
P.O. Box 2682, Bloomington, Indiana 47402-2682
www.wisdomtalespress.com

There was once a beautiful maiden named Ling Yee. She lived in Hong Kong, a fishing village on the southern coast of China. All the young men in the village wanted to marry her.

But Ling Yee loved Ching Yin, a young fisherman. She was touched by his kindness. He often helped the old men pull in their boats and haul in their fish.

The couple married and after a while a son was born. The whole village celebrated the birth. There was food, dancing, and the lighting of firecrackers.

One morning, Ching Yin and the other fishermen set out as usual. They rowed out to sea in their small, wooden sampans. By mid-afternoon, lightning flashed and thunder rumbled. Rain fell from the sky in thick sheets. The sea beat its angry fists upon the shore.

Finally, the clouds parted. The boats were drifting to land. Relieved wives ran to greet their husbands. Ling Yee asked each exhausted fisherman, "Have you seen Ching Yin?" But each shook his head.

"It was impossible to see," said one.

"The waves were so huge," cried another. "I thought I was fighting a giant sea serpent!"

The last battered sampan rolled in, but Ching Yin was not in it. Ling Yee's heart sank. She could not let herself believe that he had drowned. "Maybe he found somewhere to wait out the storm," she thought.

Every morning, Ling Yee put her baby on her back.
Then she hiked to the top of a cliff overlooking the ocean.
There she would scan the horizon for her husband. But
Ching Yin's sampan never came. At the end of each day
she would return to her hut. Her parents and the other
villagers tried to talk her into giving up her vigil.

"No," she said. "Ching Yin will come home soon."

But this went on for many moons. The men talked about the night of the terrible storm. The women lamented, "What will happen to Ling Yee and her baby?" The children whispered about the strange woman on the hill.

The young woman's parents were heartbroken over Ling Yee's grief. They pleaded with Tin Hau, the patron goddess of fishermen, for help. "Please bring Ching Yin home. Have pity on our daughter's sorrow!" they prayed.

Ling Yee's lonely figure on the cliff day after day touched
Tin Hau's heart. One day, she decided that they should
mourn no more. With a clap of her hands, Tin Hau sent a
lightning bolt to the ground. CRRACK! It turned Ling Yee
and her baby into stone.

Ling Yee now stood on top of the cliff looking out to sea. Her stony shape patiently watched for the return of her husband. The villagers began to call her the Rock Maiden. From time to time, they would lay flowers at her feet.

One day, about a year later, a stranger appeared in the village. He had a beard, scruffy clothes, and a knapsack on his back. He asked the villagers where he could find Ling Yee.

An old man stepped out of the crowd. His back was hunched and his face lined with sadness.

"You are obviously not from these parts, stranger," the old man said. "Why do you look for Ling Yee?"

The stranger put his hand on the other man's shoulder. "Do you not recognize me?" the young man asked. "I am Ching Yin. I have come home."

The astounded villagers crowded around. They wanted
to hear his story. He said that his sampan had been
overturned by ferocious waves. Finally, he found himself
washed up on the shores of a faraway village.

"I had no money and didn't know where I was. It has
taken me a year to make my way home," he explained.

The old man then told Ching Yin what had happened
to his wife and child. He pointed sadly to the rock on top
of the cliff.

Ching Yin hurried to the Rock Maiden. He stared at the stony shape of his wife and baby. Weeping bitterly, he fell to his knees.

But, high in the Heavens, Tin Hau once again took pity on this young family. With another clap of her hands, she sent a bolt of lightning through the clouds. CRRACK! It struck the Rock Maiden. The rock split open. There appeared Ling Yee and her son! Astounded, they all rushed to embrace each other.

That evening, the whole village rejoiced. Firecrackers
sparkled and popped. People danced and feasted. And songs
praising the mercy of Tin Hau floated up into the air . . .

Gently, the Queen of the Heavens gathered and folded
them into the night sky.

The Legend of the Amah Rock

The Rock Maiden is based on an old Chinese legend. The real rock is called the Amah Rock in the Sha Tin area of Hong Kong. It is a natural granite rock formation shaped amazingly like a woman with a baby on her back. It stands 50 feet high and sits on a hill 820 feet above sea level. Citizens and visitors to Hong Kong can hike up to the rock where they will have a tremendous view of Sha Tin and the surrounding hills.

Amah (prounounced *Ah-Mah*) is a Chinese word that often refers to a servant or a nanny—someone who works for another family taking care of the household and looking after the children. It is also a word that means "mother," which is probably the correct meaning for the Amah Rock as the legend is about a mother and her baby.

The legend of the Amah Rock is about a young woman who lost her fisherman husband at sea. In her grief, she climbed to the top of a hill every day with her baby on her back, patiently waiting for him to return. Tin Hau, the Goddess of the Heavens, took pity on her and turned the woman and her baby into stone (some say so her spirit can join that of her husband's, others say so she won't be sad anymore). Because of the legend, the Amah Rock is a symbol of love and loyalty to many wives and women in Hong Kong.

As a teenager growing up there, I was captivated by this story. There is a hotel in Sha Tin with a large outdoor patio and a gorgeous view of the hills, valley below, and the Amah Rock. My family would go there on weekends for lunch or afternoon tea and I'd spend the time watching the Amah Rock and willing her to come back to life. She never did, of course, but her story has always stuck with me.

Years later, when I sat down to write this story, I felt that it was too sad to end it with the young maiden being turned into a rock, so I re-envisioned the story with a happier ending—where the husband finds his way home to his loyal wife and son.

—Natasha Yim